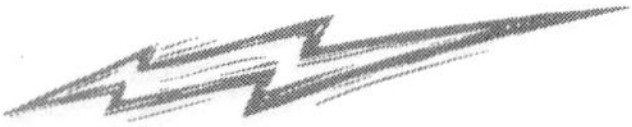

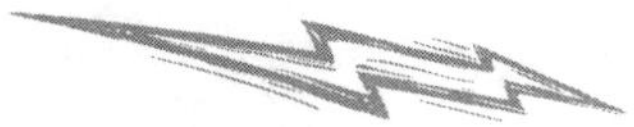

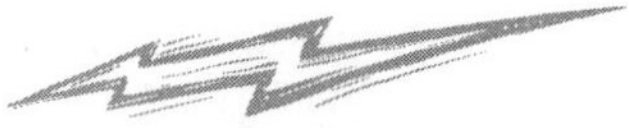

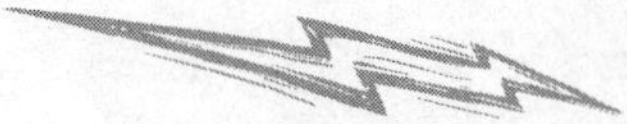

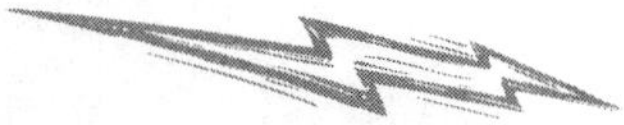

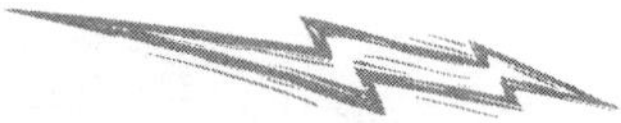

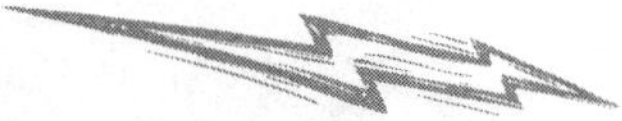

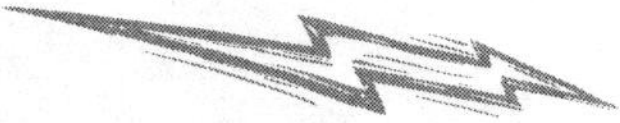

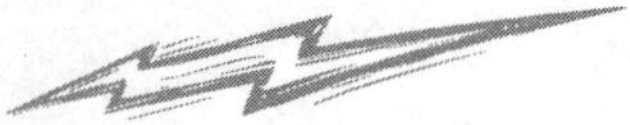

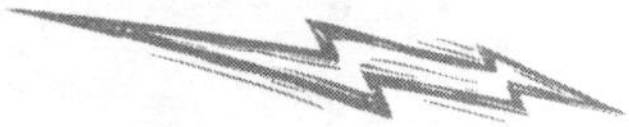

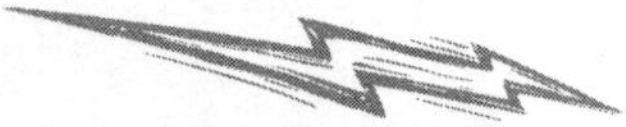

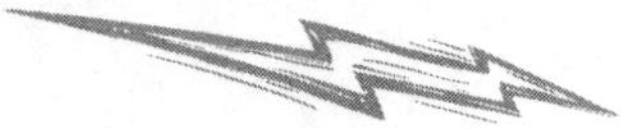

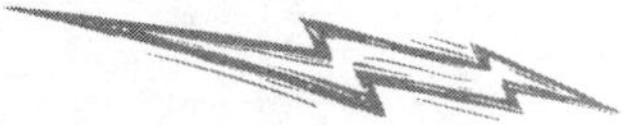

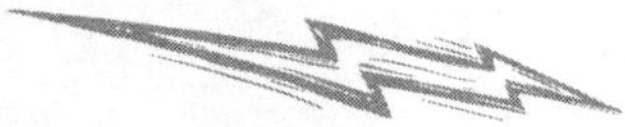

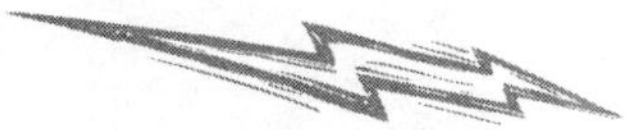

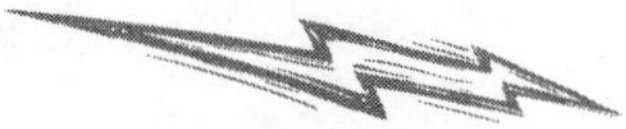

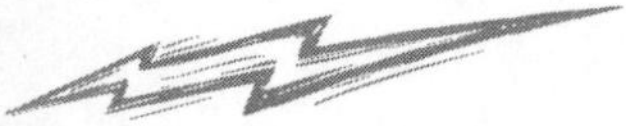

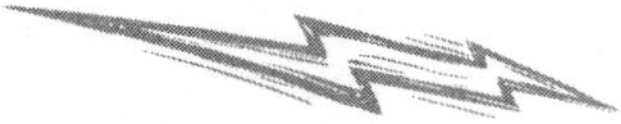

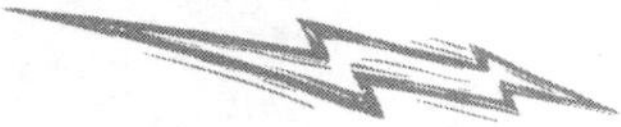

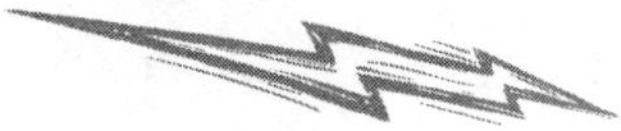

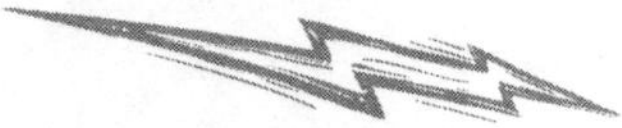

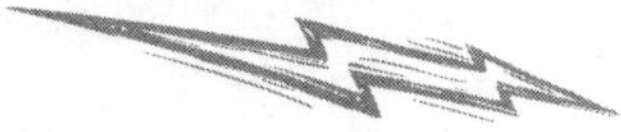

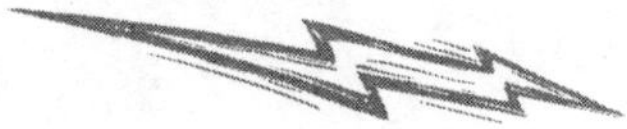

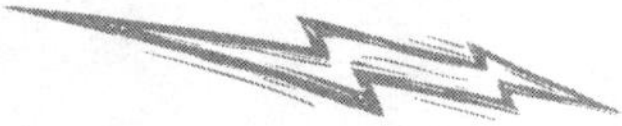

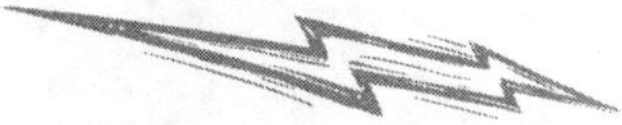

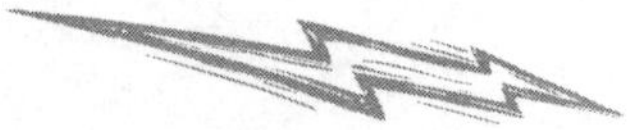

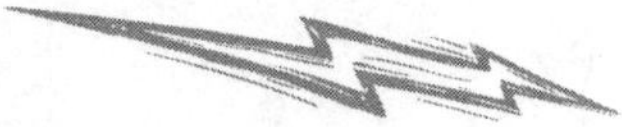

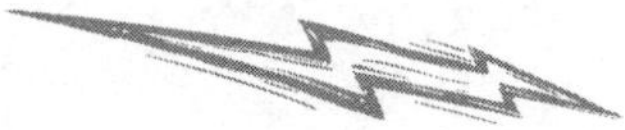

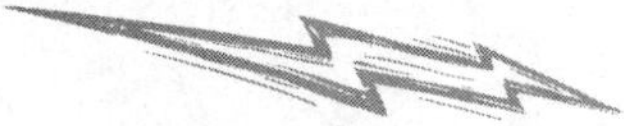

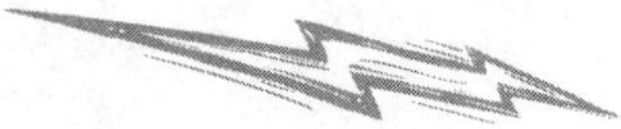

 Published by Scholastic Inc.

ISBN 0-439-23655-X
Printed in the U.S.A.
First Scholastic printing, November 2000